For Helen Mortimer

First US edition 2021
First published by Oxford University Press (UK) 2021

Library of Congress Catalog Card Number pending
ISBN 978-1-5362-1851-0

LEO 26 25 24 23 22 21
10 9 8 7 6 5 4 3 2 1

Printed in Heshan, Guangdong, China

This book was typeset in Adobe Caslon Pro.
The illustrations were done in watercolor
with physical and digital collage.

Candlewick Press
99 Dover Street
Somerville, Massachusetts 02144

www.candlewick.com

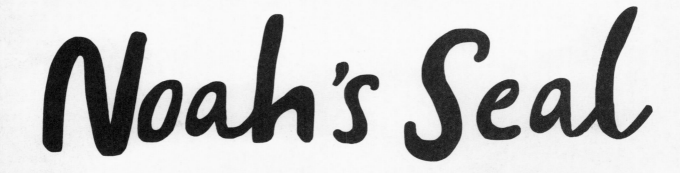

Noah's Seal

Layn Marlow

CANDLEWICK PRESS

At the edge of the wild wide sea
lies a sandy beach, where Noah sits and waits.

He waits as he did yesterday and the day before that.

"Nana, when can we go for a sail?" he asks.
"When can we go see the seals?"

"One day soon," says Nana, as always.
"I still need to fix the boat.

Why don't you play in the sand
again while you wait?"

Noah looks out to sea,
hoping to see a seal,
but Nana says they don't like
to come ashore here.

So Noah begins to dig.

As he digs, he dreams of a speckled seal
with whiskers and shining eyes.

And as he digs, the sand piles up behind him
in a big damp mound.

When Noah turns around, he gasps . . .

as he sees his very own seal!

It looks as if it's waiting for me, thinks Noah.

Just waiting to be my friend.

"Here," he says,
"I'll smooth you into shape."

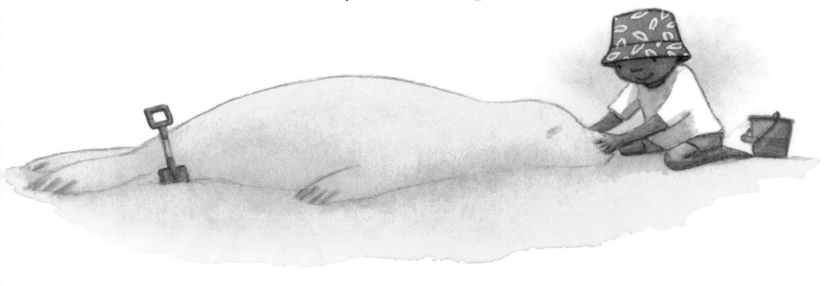

Noah finds shells for the seal's speckled back,
spiky dune grass for whiskers,

two shiny pebbles for eyes,
and a piece of seaweed for a mouth.

"There," says Noah. "Now you can see the sea."

Noah's seal smiles.

The two of them lie stretched out on the sand together.
They dream of the wild wide sea . . .

until suddenly Nana calls.

"Quickly, Noah! A storm is coming.
Let's wait in the boat until it blows over."

The wind whips up. The waves grow big,
and raindrops start to fall.

Noah has to leave his seal on the sand.

"Do you think my seal will be all right?" Noah asks.
Nana peeks out from under the tarp.

"Goodness!" she cries. "It looks like a real seal!"

"It *is* a real seal," says Noah proudly.

Nana smiles. "Then I'm sure it will be all right.
Seals like to be wet."

But when they climb out of the boat
and the storm is gone,

Noah's seal is gone too.

"It must have swum away," says Noah bravely.
"I wish I'd said goodbye."

"Never mind," says Nana kindly.
"I've finished fixing the boat, so
maybe we can go for a sail tomorrow."

"Aren't we ready to go now?" Noah asks.
But Nana is already packed and heading for home.

Then suddenly Noah cries . . .

"LOOK! Nana, look! My seal came back!"

When Nana turns around, she gasps . . .

as she sees that Noah is right!

"It looks as if it's waiting for us," says Nana.

"Waiting there, right now,
to show us the way . . .

out on the
wild wide sea!"